THE MENTORIAN

THE EGG, NECKTOR AND SOURCE-CONNECTION

THE MENTORIAN

THE EGG, NECKTOR AND SOURCE-CONNECTION

HUNI HUNFJORD

Copyright © 2017 by Watchon Publishing.

For information contact:
Kirkjuvegur 28, 230 Keflavik, Iceland
phone: +354 821 1977
http://www.hunihunfjord.com

Cover design by Huni Hunfjord
Book design, editing and formatting by Watchon Publishing
Translation by Huni Hunfjord

ISBN: 978-9935-9342-2-2
First Edition: April 2017

WHY DID I WRITE THIS BOOK?

When my five year old daughter met her five year old step brother, all hell broke loose. They mixed like water and oil or should I say not at all. If they were not screaming or crying, they were up to not good, like clogging up the kitchen sink or making a cake from the fruit basket on the kitchen table. They pulled each others hair, punched, kicked and threw things at each other. I did not know how to solve this domestic dilemma, but I knew I would not solve it by force. I truly believe one should not but fire out with more fire. The logical way for me is to sit down and figure out ways to remove all the oxygen from the room and extinguish the fire that way. Once I had pondered on the challenge for awhile I decided to tell them stories at night about a prince and a princess that were foster siblings and I made it clear that the story about the prince and the princess could possibly be about them. I allowed them to draw their own conclusion, when they asked if the stories was about them, not denying nor confirming it. In the first story the princess was kidnapped by a dragon and the prince had to find ways to help the princess. Once we were through the second story I saw great improvement in their interactions. They were both very focused on the stories and looked like they experiencing the story as there own. The next day they started to ask me for the next part of the story, way before their bedtime. This book was written to teach my foster son and my daughter to work together and to be nice to one another through teaching them by experiencing the fairy tale as if it was real. I believe this book will do the same for other kids around the world.

The Mentorian is a story for parents that want to teach their children to work together. If you want to make the story even more powerful for your children, I recommend giving the prince and princess your children's names. I believe that will increase their imagination when it comes to relating and experiencing the story as if it was written about them. Making it even easier for them to experience the story through empathy. It is my sincere belief that this story can make a difference around the world after seeing the impact with my own eyes.

Now sit back and enjoy!

TABLE OF CONTENTS

HUNI HUNFJORD

THE UNIVERSE

The prince and princess were always fighting! Sometimes they plotted together and did something they were not allowed to do, like breaking the rules. That seemed to be the only time they could be nice to one another. Every single day at least one of them would cause the other to cry. Why are they so cruel to each other? No one knew. People were wondering how come a prince and a princess behave so badly. They simply could not work together.

Their story begins when the prince's mother and the princess's father thought about ways to teach the prince and the princess to work together and to be nicer to one another. The king and queen asked the universe for help. They asked the universe to teach the prince and princess to behave better and be nicer to each other. What the parents did not know, is that the universe is always listening and he answers each time, but the answers are unpredictable, most of the time. The universe can teach us life lessons that we need to learn with the some of the most unpredictable scenarios.

THE EGG

Once upon a time, long, long ago, in a beautiful kingdom, far, far away, a prince and a princess were walking along a path in the forest nearby the castle. They were about to start arguing once again. The prince snatched the wooden stick from the princess, which she had just picked up from the path. He started to hit the branches that reached over the path with the wooden stick. The princess started crying and grabbed the stick forcefully back from the prince. Then the prince got mad and pulled the princess's hair hard and pinched her neck. She was bawling hysterically and when she caught her breath back, she picked up a rock from the path and threw it and hit the prince. Now they were both bawling hysterically on the path.

While they both stood there bawling, a light fairy sat on a mushroom near by. The light fairy was nipping at a nut and had been watching the siblings for a while. The fairy decided to step in, before things got really out of hand, like it did so often when the prince and the princess were fighting. The light fairy jumped off the mushroom and onto the path in front of the siblings and got their attention. He told them he had news of the most importance and there is a lot at stake. He explained that he would have to ask them for a very big favor. He continued explaining to them, that if they would continue on the path for awhile they would come to a huge abandoned nest nearby the path and there is an abandoned egg laying in the middle of the nest. This egg is of the utmost importance because it's the last of its kind. It is a mentorian egg. Yes, that's right, inside the egg is a potential mentorian.

A mentorian is an animal that has a body built like a muscular track race horse. He has four legs, that do not really resemble legs at all, they are more like muscular well toned arms. The back legs are wider and stronger than the front. On each of this four arms there are five fingers with powerful sharp claws on each fingers, so powerful they can easily puncture a ship and sink it. When he is running on the ground and not flying, he looks like he is running on closed fists and his running style is not unlike a horse. He has incredibly strong wings that look like the wings of an eagle. Each wings is twice as long as his whole body and head. His tail is similar to a dragon's tail. The head looks similar to a lion's head with a great beautiful friendly mane. The mouth is a little bit longer that a lion's mouth, more like a wolf's mouth. The myth states that he can breath fire and he can flap his wings so hard while flying that he can forms a tornado underneath him if he chooses to. His teeth look like a mixture between a wolf and a lion and they are considered to be made out of the strongest material on earth, stronger than diamonds. Yet no one knows exactly what that material is. There have been documented stories where a mentorian bites a sword in half that is made out of steel. The rumor is that the only thing that can kill a mentorian, is if his necktor dies or if he is poisoned.

There have been several stories written about a mentorians. Centuries ago there were many mentorians that existed but today they are becoming extinct. There are some stories that tell a tale of a mentorian and humans living side by side, but no one know if they are based on facts or fiction. The stories explain that a mentorian can connect with humans through the vibrational energy field all humans resonate with and that the connection can only be made at the moment a mentorian hatches from the egg, after that it is too late, you cannot connect with a mentorian after that. This ceremonial bonding is called the source-connection and there is no know stronger bond than the source-connection. The connection is so strong that the mentorian can sense if his necktor is in any kind of distress, no matter how far away he or she is. A necktor is a woman or man who has the source-connection with a mentorian. According to the stories, the person who source-connects with a mentorian is connected to him with this strong bond until death does them apart. The source-connection is stronger than the bond of love. The last human to source-connect with a mentorian was a great warrior known by the name of Hercules. He and his mentorian kept peace in the kingdom a thousand years ago. The kingdom was at piece until the day Hercules died as an old and happy man. According to the stories the mentorian laid beside Hercules's grave in morning until he starved himself to death. A mentorian is said to be unable to carry on living without his necktor after they have been source-connected. No man nor woman has been able to source-connect with a mentorian since then, or at least not recorded anywhere. But who knows what is really true? The children in the kingdom have been listened with passion to the tales of *Hercules and The Mentorian* for many centuries.

The light fairy had witnessed earlier that day when trophy hunters had poisoned the last living mentorian couple in the world. Thankfully the mentorians were far away from the nest so the trophy hunters did not know about the egg, therefore it is now possible to save the egg. The fairy emphasized to the prince and princess the importance to get to the egg as soon as possible to prevent the egg from loosing temperature and becoming cold. If the egg becomes completely cold, the last mentorian on earth would die. The siblings were now faced with a challenge to work together and keep the egg at body temperature until the mentorian was ready to be hatched.

The prince and princess were ready for this mission and they started immediately walking towards the nest like the light fairy has asked them to do. They got so excited about the whole thing that they started running towards the nest. When they had ran for about 10 minutes they arrived at a huge nest a few feet off the path. They climbed up and looked into the nest and saw one large egg sitting in the middle of the nest. The princess picked up the egg carefully and she felt that the egg had started to get cold already, so she put it under her coat to get it back to body temperature while they walked back to the castle. The prince and princess were now for the first time in their lives obligated to help one another or the egg would get cold and the mentorian would die and that was something they really did not want to happen. They had both been raised listening to the tales of *Hercules and The Mentorian,* but nether had ever seen such a creature with their own eyes, only pictures in books.

The next few days were very unusual for the prince and princess. They woke up earlier than usual and when they woke up, the first thing they did was to go to each others room to check on the egg. Each night they would take turns keeping the egg warm in their beds. No one in the kingdom knew how long it would take to hatch a mentorian egg, so with full enthusiasm and excitement the siblings kept on taking care of the egg both day and night, making sure to keep the egg warm. What if the egg had become too cold the day they found the egg? Then the mentorian is already dead inside the egg. They shuddered at the thought of the mentorian being dead inside the egg. They kept their spirits high and hoped for the best and kept on alternating the night watch keeping the egg warm. Tonight it is the princess's turn to take care of the egg.

THE CARPET DEMON

In the middle of the night when the princess had the egg with her, she woke up because she heard noise like someone was scratching at the window. She sat up and looked at the egg and then at the window but there was nothing to see. Her room was on the fifth floor of the castle, who could possibly be scratching at the window, this high up anyway? By the time she was almost asleep again, she heard, *scratch, scratch, scratch*, so she rose up in her bed and looked carefully around in the room. Again there was nothing to see. The princess felt uncomfortable about the whole thing, but slowly and surely she started to does off again. When she was somewhere between wake and sleep, she heard it again, *scratch, scratch, scratch*, this time she was really startled when she saw that the egg was gone!

When she had grasped the situation, the egg was really gone, she looked around in panic and saw a magic carpet flying out through the window. This meant only one thing, there was a carpet demon that had flown inside her room on the fifth floor, snatched the egg and was carrying it off. Carpet demons love eggs! They don't love them to hatch them. They love to eat them! This meant real trouble. The princess jumped out of her bed and ran as fast as she could towards the window, she stretched out trying to grab on to the carpet, but she only caught one thread. She held on tight to the thread while she watched the carpet demon fly away. She saw that the thread was slowly unraveling the carpet. The further the carpet demon flew the smaller the carpet got. The princess is clever and resourceful, therefore she realized that if she would not let go of the thread, it would lead to the carpet demon and the mentorian egg falling to the ground. From that height the egg would surely break, so she let go. The carpet demon flew far over the forest with a long thread hanging from the magic carpet.

The princess ran into the prince's room, woke the prince up and told him "the egg has been stolen, it was a carpet demon that stole it!" The prince jump out of bed and asked the princess where the carpet demon had taken the egg. She told him that she saw the carpet demon fly deep into the forest toward Black Lake, which is located in the center of the forest. They went straight to the library to see Baltasar the librarian. Baltasar is old and wise and maybe no wonder since he has read all the books in the library at least once and some more more than once. He told the siblings to find the book *Egg Trouble*. Baltasar told them that they would find good source material on carpet demons in that book, where they can be found, what they do and so forth. The prince and princess found the book, opened it up and started to read about carpet demons. They read that carpet demons are known to carry their loot to Black Lake, where they have a hearth set up to cook their stolen eggs. Carpet Demons use the water from Black Lake to boil their eggs, possibly because the lake is salty.

When the princess and prince were getting ready to head out to the forest and start looking for their egg, Baltasar warned them "you will have be extremely careful going into the forest while it is still dark outside because there are flowers that live in the forest and according to folk lure, they only travel in during night when it's dark outside. These flowers love princes and princesses. The flowers love the taste of royalty. The flowers are known by the name gorge-royal. The prince and princess headed towards the forest right away, where they devised a plan of action. When they reached the outskirts of the forest it was still dark outside. They knew they could not wait around any longer because if the egg would become cold the mentorian would die and if the carpet demon would boil the egg he would surly die as well. The princess had an epiphany and told the prince they could lay down in the swamp nearby and cover themselves completely with the mud in the swamp so the gulp-royals would not recognize that they are royalty. The prince liked the idea, so they laid down in the swamp and covered themselves with mud until only their eyes were visible. Then they started to creep slowly into the forest even though it was still dark outside.

They did not get far into the forest when they started to hear movement around them. They tried to look around and the prince whispered into the princess's ear "do you think they know we are royalty?" The princess replied "no, we look like the farmers children from the village, not like a prince and princess." They kept on walking slowly deeper into the forest and all the sudden a large flower was right in front of them. This was a huge gulp-royal.

A gulp-royal is a flower that has roots that lay on top of the ground and they can use the roots to walk on. The flower has a very large head in a similar shape of a rose with a large toothed mouth. The mouth has rows of sharp teeth similar to a shark. It looks like the gulp-royal uses red lipstick due to their noticeable strong red colored lips. They have two big green leaves on each side of their stem and one could easily think that the leaves function as arms. Both leaves are covered with small blue cilium. If you look carefully at the cilium they can be seen moving around like seaweeds in the ocean.

The gulp-royal said to the siblings "what are you doing in these parts of the forest? Don't you know this is a dangerous place to be at when it's dark outside?" They nodded their heads and the princess told the gulp-royal that they are looking for a ball they lost around here earlier this week. What the princess did not know, is that the gulp-royal have a special talent to spot a lie. When we humans tell a lie our vibrational energy changes and the gulp-royal can detect the vibrational change with their cilium. What may be even more important is that the princess did not realize that the gulp-royal have a very keen sense of smell as well. They can smell royalty. The gulp-royal asked the siblings where they were coming from and kept on asking them questions, which the princess kept on answering with one lie after another. If the prince and princess would have gazed at the flowers leaves, they would have noticed the movement of it's cilium like an ocean wave each time the princess told a lie. While they stood there talking with the flower, another gulp-royal was creeping up behind them slowly with his mouth wide open ready to swallow them whole. When the gulp-royal behind them was getting ready to strike, the prince noticed that one of his shoelaces was untied. When he bent down to tie his shoelace, he noticed the roots from the flower standing behind them, he was so startled that he screamed from the top of his lungs "RUN!" A gulp-royal has incredibly good hearing as well and therefore they can't stand much noise. When the prince yelled out loud for the princess to run, the gulp-royal became flustered right before he could swallow the princess whole. The prince and princess ran on the path as fast as they could away from the gulp-royals. They ran and ran, but the flowers could run a little bit faster than the sibling, gaining on them with each step. When the prince and princess got closer to Black Lake with the flowers in reaching distance behind them, the gulp-royals stopped following them all the sudden. It was almost like the flowers suddenly became scared of something. Could it be Black Lake it self or maybe, just maybe, the legends about the Black Lake serpent are true. Maybe there lives a monster in the lake after all.

Who knows, but the prince and princess reached Black Lake and the gulp-royals were nowhere to be seen. The sun was starting to reach out between the branches of the trees. They walked on the bank of Black Lake and saw how beautiful everything was over there. The morning sun rays dancing on the calm surface of the lake. Suddenly the prince stopped and said "look there is smoke coming from over there!" The crept slowly towards the smoke and saw the carpet demon busy doing something at the hearth. He had already put water into the pot and it was already steaming from the pot, getting close to boiling temperature. The egg laid there on the ground close to the hearth, fortunately because now the temperature of the egg should have stayed warm enough for the mentorian to be alive.

They hid behind a tree. The princess got an idea. She told the prince to show himself to the carpet demon and lure him away from the egg and she would make a run for the egg. The prince thought about it for a minute and decided to execute the idea. He ran to the bank and yelled "HEY, LOOK AT ME!". The carpet demon was startled and he immediately started to sprint towards the prince. As soon as the carpet demon left the hearth the princess jumped out from behind the tree, ran to the hearth and picked up the egg carefully and she decided in the spur of the moment to grab the magic carpet as well. When she started to run off with the egg and carpet away from the hearth the carpet demon realized that he was being played. He turned around and saw the princess running with his magic carpet. He quickly turned around and sprinted even faster this time towards the princess. He was gaining ground on her really fast because she was running slowly being careful not to drop the egg and the magic carpet did not help with her speed neither. She ran on the bank of Black Lake and when the carpet demon was just about in reaching distance from her, she threw the magic carpet into the air over the lake. The carpet demon reacted and jumped high into the air towards the lake trying to reach the carpet. He was frantically reaching for the carpet as both were flying off the bank into the lake. When carpet demons are very young they are given a carpet which is woven with a piece of their soul into the carpet and therefore the carpet has the ability to fly with the demon on top of the carpet. That is why he was so frantic about reaching the carpet because if he would loose it, he would essentially loose a part of his soul. He grabbed a hold of the carpet in the air and when he was getting ready to save himself by holding on to the carpet and flying up, a huge monster arose from the lake. The Black Lake serpent jumped out of the lake with his mouth wide open and swallowed the carpet demon whole. The stories are true then, the Black Lake serpent is real. Yummy, yummy. According to the legends the serpent loves carpet demons. The serpent likes the carpet demons for their sweet taste, just like candy.

The prince ran to the princess and they took a careful look at the egg. The temperature was fine and everything looked OK, no cracks, but they were nevertheless in shock after that morning adventure. The serpent is real. They found their way back to the path and headed towards the castle. Their moods slowly returned to normal and the feeling of joy took over like it had been for the last few days. They were happy again. When they finally reached the castle, they were completely beat and slept the whole day on the hide in front of the fireplace with the egg between them, both resting one arm on the egg.

THE NIGHT TERROR

A few days later and there seemed to be no progress with the egg. The princess and prince were getting anxious to see whether the egg would hatch or not. Tonight it is time for the prince to take care of the egg. He took the egg with him to his room, laid down on the bed with the egg and slowly started to drift into sleep. As he fell asleep he started to have a dream about Black Lake, he was standing on the bank when he heard a snickering like you might imagine how a prankster would laugh after a prank. The snickering felt so real, like it was actually not coming from the dream but instead from his room. He woke up and looked around in the room but there was nothing unusual to see. He laid back down and started to fall asleep again but before he was completely asleep he heard the snickering again, this time he was sure it came from within his room. It was like the snickering came from underneath his bed. The prince jumped out of the bed and looked underneath his bed. Nothing! Then he heard the snickering again but this time it was coming from the hallway. The prince looked at the bed and in shock noticed that the egg was gone. "What, where is it?" The egg was gone! "I can't believe it!" He looked under the cover and behind the pillows, the egg was really gone. He quickly ran into the hallway and there was nothing there. He walked back and forth in the hallway looking for the egg or some kind of clue what just happened. When he was about to return to his room he heard the snickering again but this time it came through the open window in the hallway, the sound was coming from outside the castle.

The prince hurried off to the princess and woke her up. He told her what just happened and that someone had stolen the egg while he was still in the room. They headed straight to the library to see Baltasar and told him what just happened. Baltasar told them this could possibly be a night terror. They looked puzzled at each other and said "a night terror, what is that?" Baltasar suggested a book called *Daydreaming or a Nightmare*. He continued telling the siblings that in this book they could read about a night terrors. They found the book and started to read.

A night terror is a small white rabbit that loves sunbathing during the daytime but at night she turns into a large gray hare. The hare is known for its pranks and thievery. The little white rabbit loves carrots, but only one kind that she can't resist, it's the star-carrot. The star-carrots are believed to posses supernatural ingredients and that you may only find them under a full moon in the old cemetery behind the castle by the old oak tree, which no one really knows how old the tree really is. It is believed that the star-carrots are only visible under the moon light but no one really knows if there is any truth to these tails. No one has ever been able to trade back what has been stolen by a night terror, there is a theory if one could get his hands on a star-carrot, there might be a possibility to trade with the white rabbit during daytime.

The prince and princess kept on reading until they saw that the little white rabbits can sometimes be spotted in the meadow on the south side of the forest. They can be spotted their if the sun is out because they like to stay there to sunbathe. They also read that the meadow could possibly be the only place possible to offer the rabbit to trade the loot for a star-carrot. The princess said hopelessly that they would have to find a star-carrot to even have a slight chance of getting their egg back. Baltasar told them that if the records are true then they are in luck because tonight there is a full moon.

The prince and princess grabbed a flashlight and headed outside, around the castle and towards the old oak tree by the cemetery. They walked up to the fence surrounding the cemetery and looked over and saw nothing, just grass. It was partly cloudy outside and the moon was hiding behind a cloud. After a while the moon came out but still they saw no star-carrots. They climbed over the fence and started walking around the cemetery when another cloud came to block the moon again. They saw nothing. A minute later the moon appeared again from behind the clouds and they heard movement around them. The prince asked the princess to turn off the flashlight. When she did they saw something incredible underneath the moonlight, they saw mole-gremlins jumping down into their holes all over the cemetery.

A mole-gremlin is a creature similar to a mole. They are known for their aggressiveness and that you can only see them at night. When a mole-gremlin is about to attack they growl like a dog with rabies. They see incredibly well in the dark. Many years ago there was a mole-gremlin epidemic in the kingdom. They have very crooked, ugly and decayed teeth. A mole-gremlin's mouth is so full of bacteria that if they bit a human, the human will die very soon unless he gets intravenous antibiotic treatment right away. There is only one other known way to survive their bit, that is to use extract from the leaves on the old oak tree. It is the only tree that carries the antidote in it's leaves.

At first they got scared but they decided continue searching anyway, pushing through the fear. They decided to continue and step outside their comfort zone since they had a very good reason to find a star-carrot. Their why, was that they loved the mentorian so much, that they were willing do things to get him back, that they would normally not be able or willing to do. When their eyes got adjusted to the darkness with only the moon light above them, they saw the most beautiful leaves they ever seen, sticking half way out of the ground. The leaves were sparkling in the moon light like stars in the sky. It looked like magic.

The prince and princess started to move towards the leaves and when the prince reached down and grabbed the leaves getting ready to pull them out of the ground, a mole-gremlin came running at them, full speed. He hurried to pull the leaves up and out of the group and as soon as the carrot came out of the ground the mole-gremlin snatched the carrot right out of his hand and jumped down another hole in the cemetery with the carrot. They looked at the ground and it was covered with star dust from the carrot and it sparkled so beautifully in the moon light. Then another cloud covered the moon and the it was like the dust had never been there, completely dark and they saw nothing for a minute. When the moon appeared again they saw another set of sparkling leaves sticking out of the ground about 20 feet away from them. The princess told the prince to hold the flashlight and get ready and she reached down, grabbed the leaves, ready to pull the carrot out of the ground. Another mole-gremlin came at them, full speed. She got a solid hold of the leaves and as soon as she was ready to pull the carrot she shouted at the prince "TURN ON THE LIGHT!" He turned on the flashlight and the leaves disappeared but the princess could still feel them. The mole-gremlins have excellent night vision and therefore when the strong light hit the mole-gremlin's eyes he got blinded and he started screaming out of agony. He saw nothing and ran out of control in circles in the cemetery wailing. The princess pulled the invisible leaves and the carrot came out of the ground. It was so beautiful. Then the moon got covered once again by another cloud.

Big trouble! When the moon appeared again the siblings were surrounded by, over forty, mole-gremlins and they all were all growling. The prince and princess both remembered that the mole-gremlins are very aggressive and they growl right before they are ready to attack. The siblings became extremely scared. The prince tried to shine the flashlight into their eyes but there were simply too many of them. They turned around and started running as fast as they could towards the fence. It became completely dark, because not only did another cloud covered the moon as they began to run, but the prince also dropped the flashlight in panic into the high grass. They ran anyway, because they were so scared. They both hit the fence with their hips at such speed that they completely tipped over the fence, like a seesaw. Now they were both laying on their backs in the grass on the other side of the fence in total darkness, listening the flock on growling mole-gremlins behind them. The prince took the princess's hand and they both curled up in the grass getting ready for the attack. Both had one hand covering the top of their head, protecting themselves. After what seemed like a long time but really was only about ten seconds, the moon came out again. All the crazed mole-gremlins were now foaming at the mouth trying to force their way outside the fence to attack them. The prince and princess slowly stood up and saw that none of the mole-gremlins were getting thought the fence. The mole-gremlins then started one by one jumping into their holes all over the cemetery and the prince and princess froze with fear. Most likely they are digging their way under the fence to the siblings. The prince and princess were in big trouble when one of the mole-gremlins dug his way though the ground underneath the fence and came up right beside the siblings. The mole-gremlin ran full speed at them and bit the princess. When he tried to bite the princess his teeth fell out of his mouth. Then in matter of second the prince and princess watched the mole-gremlin grow old and finally falling to the ground into a pile of dust. Puff, just like that, the wind blew his dust away.

Many years ago there was an epidemic of mole-gremlins in the kingdom. One of the most powerful wizards in the world was summoned to save the kingdom from this epidemic. The wizard put a spell on the cemetery so that the mole-gremlins could not survive outside cemetery, if they breach the fence they grow old very fast and die.

What a relief for the sibling, but they knew that their journey had just began, they had not gotten their mentorian egg back yet. Once they arrived back at the castle, they tried to lay down for a bit to get some sleep but both of them just laid in their bed staring at the ceiling thinking about the trauma filled night, being unable to sleep, but that's understandable after a terrifying night like that. They had one star-carrot which gave them hope that they could possibly reunite with the mentorian in the morning. They lied silently awake together and waited for the sun to come out.

A few hours later the sun started to rise. The prince and princess took the star-carrot with them and headed towards the meadow on the south side of the forest. When they arrived, they started to look for a little white rabbit anywhere but there were no rabbits around. After awhile they started to give up hope and were slowly walking across the meadow towards the castle when the spotted white fur between the tussocks. The started to approach the rabbit "oh, look how cute and soft it looks" said the princess while they slowly advanced towards the rabbit. They both had to restrain themselves from thinking about just cuddling the cute little white rabbit. They had to remind themselves, that they were there to trade with the rabbit and not there to cuddle nor to pat the rabbit. Right before they reached the rabbit the prince fell over a tussock and startled the rabbit so much that she jumped into the air, then ran in a couple of circles and finally jumped into a hole close by. The prince and princess ran to the hole and spoke gently and politely down the hole "hallo, can we talk with you?" They waited but no answer. They tried to raise their voice a little and said "excuse us, but do you by any change have an egg that we are looking for? The egg is light gray with green speckles. This egg is very dear to us." Still no answer and no movement. "We have a star-carrot!" said the princess softly and hopelessly.

The prince and princess gave up hope and turned away from the hole, it was probably not the rabbit who stole the egg anyway. When they turned around the rabbit stood directly in front of them with a surprised look on it's face. The rabbit stood up right, on her back legs and stared baffled at the siblings. "Do you really have a star-carrot? Can I see it?" said the rabbit. The princess reached into her coat pocket and pulled out the carrot. The rabbit's eyes doubled in size and she stuck her tongue out and licked the drool off her lower lip. "Do you have our egg?" asked the prince. The rabbit started to reach her front paws towards the star-carrot and when the princess noticed it, she quickly pulled the carrot back and put it back into her coat pocket. They noticed the obvious disappointment on the rabbit's face and it's eyes shrunk back to normal. It was like the rabbit had gone

somewhere else in it's mind while looking at the star-
carrot and now it's focus turned to the prince and the
rabbit said the prince with a surprising tone of voice;
"What? What did you just say?" The prince replied;
"Do you have the egg we are looking for?" The rabbit
looked at them back and forth for a few seconds and
then skipped right past the siblings and into the hole
without replying. The prince and princess both
shrugged their shoulders looking puzzled at each
other. After a short while the rabbit returned from the
hole with the mentorian egg. "Are you looking for this
egg?" she said. "Yes, exactly, that's the egg we are
looking for, do you want to trade?" asked the prince.
The rabbit held the egg tightly while stroking it and
replied "No, I love this egg. It's mine!" The siblings did
not understand, the rabbit seems to keen on the
carrot before, why doesn't she want to trade the egg
now. The prince and princess both knew that no one
had ever gotten a night terror to trade it's stolen
goods before and maybe this explains why, they are
simply not interested in a trade. "Do you want to
trade?" asked the princess once more. The rabbit
shock it's head, turned around and headed towards
the hole. The quick thinking princess reached into her

pocket and pulled out the star-carrot. The rabbit stopped and she started sniffing into the air, like she smelled the carrot, she turned back around. When she saw the carrot, her eyes doubled in size again. The rabbit carefully laid down the egg, not taker it's eyes of the carrot and started to walk towards the star-carrot raising it's front paws up, zombie like. It was walking upright on it's back legs with it's arms and paws stretching towards the carrot. "Do you want to trade?" asked the princess. The rabbit slowly kept on moving closer to the carrot like she was in some kind of a trans. The princess suggested with her other hand to the prince to go and take the egg while the rabbit was out off touch with reality. The prince walked to the egg and slowly picked it up and held it firmly against his body while keeping an eye on the strange rabbit. The rabbit kept getting closer and when she was within reaching distance from the egg the princess handed her the star-carrot. The rabbit took the carrot slowly from the princess with both front paws, which looked more like hands really. She put the star-carrot directly into it's mouth and started to chow down the carrot with enthusiasm. As it was eating the carrot, its eyes grew even larger and it's pupils became dilated. After a very short while the rabbit had finished the whole carrot. The rabbit started to slacken, it looked like all the bones in it's body had turned into jelly. The rabbit slowly went limp down to the ground and rolled over on her back and started to laugh. The rabbit laughed and laughed and laughed. She looked straight up and watched the clouds in sky pass by, it looked like the rabbit was experiencing it's best day ever. It's laughter was soft like it was difficult to laugh or that it was to lazy to laugh. The rabbit was in euphoria. The sibling both thanked the rabbit for the trade. The rabbit just kept on chuckling softly. "Is our business concluded?" asked the prince. After a short while when the rabbit had not said anything, the princess said "star-carrot!" The rabbit then slowly moved it's head towards the princess and kept on laughing. Somehow through the rabbit's laughter both the prince and princess understood the slight movement of the head, as nodding in agreement. Their business was done there! They had retrieved their precious egg back.

The sibling were happy as they headed back to the castle with the mentorian egg, which seemed to be at perfect temperature. The rabbit had obviously taken good care of the egg. The rabbit must have really loved the egg like it said. Tonight it is the princess's turn to take care of the egg.

THE BALD CERBERUS

Francis has been the head chief of the castle for many years now. Francis is originally from France. Very few people in the castle know anything about Francis or what he did before joining the castle's staff. Francis is considered a very good chief, he is conservative, stays out of people's business and keeps to himself for the most parts.

Francis wasn't always a chief, many years ago when he was a young man he was attending one of the best art universities in France, he had his heart set on becoming a world famous oil painting artist. When he was about half way through with this studies, a man approached him. This man had a very deep voice and was wearing a black trench coat. The man asked Francis if he could paint a painting from him. Francis like so many other students was completely broke at the time, he was considering at the time to drop out of school. He was excited about an opportunity to be able make some extra money on the side, while attending school and possibly being able to continue his schooling. Francis went by his real name back then, Gastone. The man who approached Gastone wanted him to paint a replica of a world famous painting. Gastone did not understand at the time why someone would want the same painting that already existed at a museum in France. Nevertheless, Gastone did what the man asked for. He was handsomely rewarded for the job which meant that Gastone could carry on with his studies. Very soon after the job, Gastone found out that the trench coated man was a skillful art thief. He had stolen the original painting from the museum and replaced it with Gastone's replica. Gastone was devastated when he found out that he had become an accessory to a crime, stealing one of the most famous paintings in history.

Roughly about one year later the trench coated art thief arrived at Gastone's door steps once again and he had another job for him. At the time Gastone was even broker than the first time he saw the man. He could not even afford to buy himself a proper dinner, since all his money was invested in his education, therefore it was very difficult decision for Gastone to make, whether he should work for the art thief or not. It only took one week for starving for Gastone to reason himself into why he should take the job. Gastone called the art thief and told him he would do the job but he wanted more money this time. The man quickly replied to him and told Gastone he would double the fee from the previous job, with one condition. Gastone would work for the art thief when called upon from now on, even with short notice.

From this day forth Gastone was working as a skillful art counterfeiter. Within six months Gastone had left school and was working full time counterfeiting paintings and partying. He was getting a lot of money, he could do what he pleased and sometimes he would get a priceless original painting as a payment for counterfeiting multiple other paintings.

After a few years of counterfeiting, the police was on Gastone's trail. The police had enough evidence to declare Gastone as the most wanted counterfeiter in the world. At that moment Gastone's life was turned upside down. He was not only wanted in France but in the whole world. Gastone stashed all the valuables he could with short notice, all over the world in secure locations, only he knew about. He changed his name from Gastone to Fransis with counterfeit documents and fled France. A few weeks later he got a position at the castle as a waiter and he continued to worked for two years as a waiter until one day the head chef got sick and Fransis had to fill in as the head chef while he was recovering. He quickly proved to be a very good chief and since that day he has worked at the castle as the head chef. No one in the kingdom knows that the head chef at the castle is really the most wanted counterfeiter in the world.

That morning when Fransis was serving the prince and princess breakfast, he started to politely ask the siblings about the egg that they had been taking care of for a few weeks now. They told him about all the adventures and dangers they had encountered while taking care of the mentorian egg. Fransis went into the kitchen and he felt alive for the first time for a long time, he was excited. His emotions were so strong he could not help himself, so he made some inquiries and quickly found out that the last mentorian egg in the world is priceless. Fransis had heard the stories about this great art collector in the next kingdom. This art collector Mustafa was the king of that kingdom and he lived in the most expensive castle in the world. In the south part of his castle was the most valuable art collection in the world. Mustafa had collected all kinds of art pieces from all over the globe, which most of them where so valuable that no one could possibly afford to buy them, that is to say if they would be put up for sale in the first place. Around lunch time that day Fransis had sent a carrier pigeon to the village near by, to racketeer he knew. The racketeer had a cousin in Mustafa's kingdom that could get an anonymous message to Mustafa that he could possibly get his hands on a mentorian egg and add to his collection, the last of it's kind possibly still alive. It took about four hours until Fransis received an offer for the egg. The amount of money Mustafa offered was enough to build a brand new castle. Fransis was so alive now and excited about the deal. Around dinner time Fransis was ready to take action. He asked the prince and princess to help him after the dinner, to retrieve the chocolate budding. Once they arrived in the kitchen with the egg, he asked them to go into the walk-in-freezer and get the pudding. They carefully laid the egg on a chair in the kitchen and went into the freezer. When they returned with the pudding, Fransis had painted a crack on the egg. Since Fransis was a very skillful counterfeiter, he had no problem painting a very realistic crack on the egg. Fransis wailed softly "I can't believe it, the egg is cracked." He grabbed the egg and showed the sibling the crack and was very careful not to touch the paint, as it was still wet. Fransis said with a very sad voice "I am so sorry but the mentorian is dead." The prince and princess almost had a nervous breakdown. "I can't believe it." wailed the princess as she started to bawl with grief. A second later the prince started bawling as well. They were crushed, sad beyond what words could describe. Fransis comforted them as he could and let them into the dining room to the kind and queen. He assured the kids he would take the egg and bury it next to the old oak tree by the cemetery. The siblings could not say anything, they could not speak for their grief was so overwhelming. They had endured so much protecting the egg and all for nothing! They felt like losers, not being capable of protect the egg.

The following days were hard for the prince and princess. They only exited their rooms to get food and then returned to their rooms to keep grieving the mentorian. Each morning they would walk to the old oak tree and lay out new wand of flowers on the mentorian grave, where Fransis had buried the egg.

Five days later an invitation card arrived to the castle, the queen, king, prince and princess were invited to attend the Mustafa's annual art display. The king suggested to the queen that they needed to take the prince and princess there because they needed a distraction from their grief. The following day they all traveled in the beautiful white horse carriage to Mustafa's kingdom. There was no way to talk to the prince or princess during their travel. Their tears would not stop pouring down their cheeks.

Once they all arrived at Mustafa's art display, they were greeted with catering and live music. The prince and princess walk through the art display stooped down and sad, looking at the ground and not the art work. The only reason they were there is because the queen and king did not give them an alternative. When they had walked for awhile through the art display they arrived at a hall with the a sign above the door that said "Mustafa's most valuable live art piece." They walked into the hall and saw a big display case sitting in the middle of the hall. The hall was dark with dim lights in the black curved ceiling, it looked like they were standing outside in the middle of the night looking up at the stars in the clear sky. Red light was shining from the display case, it was an incubator box. They could not have been more surprised when they approach the box and saw what was inside. The mentorian egg was inside. Their hearts stopped beating for a brief second. They stared into the box then at each other and then into the box again. They noticed that the painted crack had dripped down the egg. It was obviously paint. There was no question about it, this was their mentorian egg. They became filled with hope for a split second, then they realized that they would probably never get it back. Unless, they could plot a way to steal it back. The stories of Mustafa were not very nice at all. In the past when people had told Mustafa that he had their art in his museum, he would literally flip out, he would loose his temper because he bought each art piece for a great deal of money. Mustafa was not a thief. Yet that does not mean that he did not get tricked into buying stolen art by a person who had originally stolen the art piece, but he could not accept that idea nor admit it. The last oil painting he bought little over a year ago was painted by a famous living artist. The artist so happened to be at his art display that year and saw his piece hanging on the wall in the art display gallery. The painter addressed Mustafa and told him that he had a stolen oil painting in the museum. The painter demanded that Mustafa would return him the painting right away. Mustafa reacted with rage and had the painter hanged for accusing the kind of thievery. The prince and princess knew this story all to well and because they were now thinking clearly, they knew the only way they could get the egg back, would be to steal it back.

Mustafa had the staff make sleeping arrangements for the queen, king and the sibling in his castle. They planned on eating breakfast together and then heading back to their kingdom the following day. Now the sibling were in a dilemma. How could they possibly steal the egg. Once the art display closed, the prince and princess headed to Mustafa's library looking

for any documentation on the museum. They found a
book about the museum and read that this was the
only museum in the world that had never been
breached, nothing had ever been stolen from this
museum. The reason is most likely because of the
night watch at the museum, it is guarded by a bald
cerberus. A few years back the museum was targeted
by a couple of thieves that tried to break into the
museum. No one really knows what happened to the
thieves but they were never ever seen again. This
story is known to most of the kingdom but no one
knows if it is really true.

The two headed bald cerberus is an animal with a body similar to a boar. The skin er rough and on it's back there are hundreds of sharp quills like on a porcupine. The theory is that the bald cerberus can shoot them by holding his breath. The quills are very poisonous and will kill a grown man in a few hours. A bald cerberus is a two headed beast. The heads are somewhat similar to an owl in the way that it can rotate the each head a whole circle. Both heads have a bald spot on the top of the head and that's where the name comes from. The mouth is similar to a tiger but the face is flatter, closer to an owl. He has great night vision and moves around quickly. He has a hairy tail similar to a fox which he can use to detect the energy vibration we humans send out all the time.

The prince and princess also found a book in the library about the bald cerberus written by Mustafa himself, although he probably had one of his servant write it for him. In the book they found information about the bald cerberus. They are very loyal to their owner and he has very few weaknesses that have been documented. There is a theory that his senses can be thrown off by playing music, specifically on the piano. The vibration from the note being played mess up the bald cerberus senses, making it hard to use the tail for picking up vibrations from humans and his night vision gets blurry but that is just a theory. There has only been one bald cerberus tamed in the world that people know of and therefore the sibling could only get their hands on facts about the him written by Mustafa himself. It took Mustafa many years and many trainers to be able to train this one bald cerberus.

There are no documents stories about an adult encountering a bald cerberus in the wild and surviving. There has been one encounter documented and it was when a farmer's daughter and son were hunting in the forest one day. They were from a poor farm and were in the forest hunting squirrels. Their hunt was successful and on their way home with three squirrels, they found themselves confronted by a bald cerberus. It was getting dark outside when they stumbled on the bald cerberus laying beside a bush. He jumped up and headed towards the kids and started to make a sound with high pitched frequency that only children can hear. When humans grow older then we start to loose our ability to hear certain sounds with high pitched frequency, and therefore it is concluded that only children can hear the bald cerberus when he is about to attack. The children stiffened with fear and when the bald cerberus came closer to them the boy reacted in fear by throwing the squirrels towards him. The high pitched frequency sound stopped and he started to eat the squirrels. The children ran as fast as they could back home and lived to tell this tale. This is the only known and documented escape from encountering a bald cerberus in the wild.

The prince asked the princess if she was still taking lessons on the old piano in the big living room back home at the castle. She told him that she had not been taking lessons for awhile but a few weeks ago she sat down at the piano and she had not forgotten anything she had learned. They sat down and wrote on a piece of paper the plan for the night, what they were planing to do to be able to steal the egg. The siblings learned at an early age that everything you write down is more likely to play out just like you write it. The prince wrote down that he would go into the woods before it got dark and catch some squirrels so they could use them as a distraction for the bald cerberus while they steal the egg.

It was now middle of the night and dark, the princess had been in the kitchen earlier that evening and found some papers there which she had taken. She damped the papers with water and balled up with her hands into a replica of the egg, as close to it as she could. She planned on replacing the egg with the ball of papers which was now dry and hard. The paper ball did resemble the egg somewhat in the dark, good enough to buy them time to get away with the plan. The sibling waited one hour after they stopped hearing people still up and about in the castle to make their move. They started to sneak silently through the hallways with the paper ball and two squirrels, that the prince caught earlier that evening. They finally arrived at the entrance of the art museum in the south part of the castle.

They opened the door carefully and looked inside. It was pretty dark in the first hall. In the first hall there was a piano art collection piece which they hoped still worked. The princess would have to reach the other side of the hall to be able to start paying the piano before the bald cerberus would attack them, or even worse, kill them. She started to move slowly across the floor towards the piano, when she started to hear a high pitched frequency sound coming from outside the hall. The sound seemed to be moving closer to them. Now the sound seemed to be coming from within the hall they were in, and it seemed to be coming at the princess at an incredible speed. The prince was following the princess very closely but stopped and froze when he saw in the dim light a shadow figure moving towards them. The prince assumed that this must be the bald cerberus. He took the squirrels and threw them towards the moving shadow being. The high pitched frequency sound stopped and they could hear the bald cerberus chewing on the squirrels. The prince hurried to the princess. Now they did not have much time, how long does a bald cerberus take to eat two squirrels anyway? He pushed the princess into the seat in front of the piano, opened it up and whispered to the princess to start paying and took the paper ball from her. The princess started playing and thankfully the piano still worked. The prince quickly moved through a couple of display halls and into the hall were the egg was kept. He headed straight to the display opened it and swapped out the egg for the paper ball. He knew he had little time so he hurried back to the hall where the princess was playing soft piano music. He put his hand on to her shoulder and felt how damp she was. She had starting to sweat a lot after she stopped hearing the bald cerberus chewing on the squirrels. He was wandering around the room making that awful high pitch frequency sound again. He was trying find them and attack. The music seemed to be working, his senses were off. How in the world should they proceed getting the egg outside the room now? The princess will have to stop playing once they head towards the door, what then? The bald cerberus was now on the other side of the piano, moving slowly but surly closer to them, he was searching without his night vision and his highly sensible tail, not being able to locate them precisely.

The prince got an idea. He still had three pebbles in his pocket from the evening when he was catching the squirrels. He was a pretty accurate shot with the pebbles. He whispered into the princess's ear that she should take the egg now and go outside and he would play something until she was clear outside the hall. He played three notes over and over, C,E,G. The princess made it outside the room and he kept on playing the same three notes and had the three pebbles in his other hand. The bald cerberus had moved along the piano and was now right next to the prince. It's now or never the prince thought to himself. He stopped playing and took two big steps backwards from the piano. Once he stopped playing the piano the bald cerberus's senses returned to normal and he took a leap towards the prince and at the same time the prince threw one of the pebbles towards the piano. The pebble flew and landed directly on one of the notes and the bald cerberus's senses were shocked for that brief moment making him miss the prince by a hair, sliding on the glossy floor past him. The prince

took two more steps backwards and at that moment
the bald cerberus's senses returned to normal again.
The bald cerberus clawed the floor as he turned
around still sliding in the opposite direction creating a
high screeching sound when his claws pierced the
floor. The bald cerberus regained his momentum and
jumped at the prince, which had just thrown the
second pebble at the piano. Luckily the pebble hit
another note stunning the senses again and the prince
bend down as the bald cerberus flew over his head
barely missing him. Two more steps backwards and
the prince threw the last pebble towards the piano.
The prince was sweating profusely from the adrenaline
in his body and as a result the pebble was damp and
his hand. Right next to the prince the bald cerberus
was clawing the floor once more with all his senses
back to normal. Once the bald cerberus has turned
around facing the prince, the pebble hit the top of the
piano, bouncing again on it and finally hitting the floor,
he missed. The bald cerberus was right next to the
prince, he held his breath and shot all the quills of his
back. The prince felt the princess grabbing his scruff
and pull him out the door. As he was being pulled out
the door he felt one of the poisoned quills hitting his

thigh. They both made it outside the hall and closed the door right before the bald cerberus could get though the door. The prince felt the pain from the quill spread all over his body in a matter of seconds and his eyes rolled back in his head as he fainted.

The princess tried to wake up the prince without luck, he was completely lifeless on the floor. She sat him up against the wall in the hallway, took the egg and placed it in a leather chair sitting in front of a fireplace nearby and covered it with a blanket. The egg should be fine there for a few hours and the temperature should be OK as well. Then she lugged the prince upstairs to her bedroom and laid him lifeless on the bed. She pulled the cover over him and laid with him the rest of the night.

The princess lugged the lifeless prince early the next morning into the white beautiful horse carriage and situated him as though he was sleeping, by leaning him with one arm over the egg which she placed right next to him, both covered with a blanket. The princess then went to the breakfast table and told everyone that the prince had been sick during the night and would not be joining them this morning. The princess was very nervous that Mustafa would have already heard what went down during the night at the museum, but thankfully he did not mention a thing, so far anyway. When Mustafa was seeing everyone off once the breakfast was over, one of his servant came crashing into the dining hall and told Mustafa that he had some very important news to tell him. Thankfully Mustafa hated to be interrupted so his reaction were to yell at the servant and tell him off in front of everyone for interrupting him while he was speaking. He told the servant to go outside and wait until the guest were gone and then he could come and tell him the news, he also told the servant if he would ever interrupt him like that again there would be serious consequences. When Mustafa had said his farewell's, the queen, king and princess, headed straight out to their beautiful white horse carriage and headed home.

The king and queen thought that the prince was sick from grieving so much and that he was beginning to become delirious from exhaustion. He was so out of it, that one might assume he had been poisoned. A few hours later the carriage was riding in their own kingdom, when the prince started to move his eyes around. The princess noticed this and tried to connect with him. The only thing he could muster out was incoherent "wee, weeeet, wettt, wet." He kept on repeating this over and over again. The princess lifted up the blanket and looked under it and saw that his pants were wet. The princess thought to herself this is most likely blood from the quill hitting his thigh. When she pulled the blanket all the way off she saw that this was not blood but a clear fluid on his pants. She touched the fluid and smelled it. She had never smelt any fluid like that. It smelt like a mixture of wasabi and ginger root, or somewhere there between. The smell was pretty strong. The prince looked like he was slowly getting his strength back. What's going on, is he getting better, is he being cured?

When they arrived at the castle the prince felt good enough to be supported by his sister into the castle. The prince and princess carried the egg between them under the blanket and slowly went up to his room. He sat down carefully on his bed and the prince sighted "What happened?" The princess told him what happened and that he had been shot with a poison quill when the bald cerberus shot all his quills all over the hall. She continued to explain to him that he was very lucky to survive the night. She asked him to show her the leg. He pulled up his pant leg all the way to where the quill hit his thigh. The thigh was covered in the clear liquid. He asked her what that was and she replied that she did not know. The strange thing was neither of them saw any marks nor quill in the leg. What was going on? They pulled the blanket off the egg and saw that the egg was cracked, for real this time. The clear liquid was from the egg. The liquid must have healing powers, it saved his life.

The mentorian egg was broken. Was the mentorian dead or maybe, just maybe, he was about to hatch?

THE SOURCE-CONNECTION

No one knew what happened to Fransis. He was gone and not trace of him anywhere. The castles was is need of a new head chief now. The prince and princess sat in his room on his bed watching the egg as it dripped clear fluid on the bed. They hoped for the best. They were emotionally drained from the museum's adventure the past night. The stared at the egg feeling powerless, all they could do was watch and wait. They sat there quietly staring at the egg when the egg suddenly tipped to the side. They raised it back up and two second later it tipped to the side again. They could hear some kind of fluid movement inside the egg, like something was moving inside of it. They started to smile. Their smile turned into a grin, they could not help but feel so alive at that moment, all their efforts were about to pay off. They placed their hands on the egg and could feel the movement inside, it was obvious, the mentorian was alive. He was getting ready to hatch. They sat like this for awhile, feeling the egg with a gigantic smile on their faces. They were ecstatic.

All the sudden they heard a loud sound as another crack formed in the egg. Then another and another until the egg was completely covered in cracks. Finally the mentorian's little cute snout came peaking through the egg shell. "Oh, look how cute he is" said the princess as a tear of joy ran down her face. The prince's and princess's emotions were so great at this moment that it felt like the air inside the room had thickened. Slowly but surly the mentorian's head came out of the shell. They could not wait any longer and started to help him out by using their hands to break the shell open. Finally their mentorian was completely outside the egg. Finally!

The prince started to wipe the liquid of the mentorian with the blanket. The princess watched and all the sudden she got shocked, she froze. When she finally caught her breath again she screamed of the top of her lungs "STOP, STOP!" The princess has almost forgotten that this was the only moment a person can form the source-connection with a mentorian. The person who wants to form the source-connection and become a necktor to the mentorian must lick the fluid of the mentorian, while he is freshly hatched from the egg.

These kind of bonds are known thought out the animal kingdom, for example during lambing season. When the sheep has given birth to the lamb, she licks the fluid of the lamb and forms a bond with the lamb by doing so. An example of how important this bonding is, when a sheep has only given birth to one lamb and another sheep to three lambs, it's common that the farmer takes one of the tripled lambs and puts it behind the sheep with only one lamb. The farmer then smears the amniotic fluid on both the lambs and then presents the lambs to the sheep. If the sheep licks both the lambs, she thinks they are hers and will take care of them both as her own.

"We have to lick some of the fluid of the mentorian if we want to form the source-connection. If we want to become his necktors." said the princess. The prince stopped wiping him with the blanket and without thinking about whether the fluid tastes bad or not, they both started to lick him. Yes indeed the fluid tasted awful, they became nauseated by the taste of the viscous fluid. It seemed impossible to swallow any of it. They did not care because they love the mentorian. When they finally managed to swallow a little bit of the viscous fluid, the mentorian started to shake, almost like he was being electrocuted. He started to make a sound similar to what a purring cat makes. As soon as he started to shake the sibling froze, they could not move, they stiffened up. A few seconds later they started to shake as well. It looked like they had completely lost control of all their motor functions. They shook for awhile but then started to calm down slowly and finally loosing touch with reality. Their eyes rolled back in their heads and they both passed out on the bed.

Several hours later, the following morning when they woke up the mentorian was dry and he was laying between them curled up like a dog or a cat does when sleeping. They both had their left hand on top of the mentorian's back. When looking at them from above they kind of looked like they had been placed there carefully to form the symbol of Yin and Yang. The prince and princess laid on each side of the mentorian curled around him. "This is the greatest day of my life." said the princess and the prince nodded his head in agreement. They slowly woke up and both felt a sharp pain in their left hand, which was laying on top of the mentorian's back. The princess stood up and walked to the bathroom. She looked into the mirror and saw that all her veins were visible, from her heart through the shoulder and almost to her elbow on the left side. They were red with a black outline like a living tattoo. She stared into the mirror and saw that the necktor symbol was moving. She saw her veins get bigger and smaller as her heart pumped blood though them. She kept staring into the mirror and she knew that there was no turning back now. The prince and princess were now officially source-connected to the mentorian and had become his necktors. The source-connection lasts a lifetime and is a stronger bond than love!

IN CLOSING

Dear reader, thank you for purchasing and reading The Mentorian. I hope you enjoyed the story as much as my children did and as much I have enjoyed creating and writing it. This book has covered the first part of the journey, that the prince and princess will encounter with the mentorian. In the next book we will see how the siblings handle the mentorian and if they will be successful in training him. Are there any more dangers that lay ahead for the prince and princess? Are there any monsters, creatures or demons perhaps that want to get their hand on a young mentorian? Are there any human threats they will face as they try to gain the mentorian's trust and loyalty. When the source-connection has been formed, is it then by default that the mentorian will obey it's necktor? What does a mentorian eat? What do the sibling have to do to ensure that the mentorian will be all that he can be? Is it possible to raise a mentorian to be a coward?

I hope you found this story interesting enough to continue as we publish the next part of the journey.

Thank you so much for joining us on this adventure. May you prosper and stay grateful all the time and I hope you will tap into your empathy and treat others like you would like to be treated yourself, especially how you treat your siblings.

Sincerely, the author,

Huni Hunfjord.

THE AUTHOR HUNI HUNFJORD

Huni Hunfjord is the author of *Sleeping Habits and Routines, Top 1% Parents Raise Top 1% Children, The Mentorian, Our Road without Boundaries* and Founder of the Watchon brand and Focus Gym ♡♡ Be you! As a father of three, children and entrepreneurship are core to his life. Huni loves creating apps, music videos, new ventures, coaching and interactive stories centered around children that parents can use to help them grow and develop into the best possible version of themselves. This book has been created for parents to inspire their children to work together through the children experiencing the story as their own.

OTHER BOOKS BY HUNI HUNFJORD

Sleeping Habits and Routines

Top 1% Parents Raise Top 1% Children

Our Road without Boundaries

LEARN MORE ABOUT HUNI HUNFJORD

http://amazon.com/author/hunihunfjord

http://HuniHunfjord.com

http://IcyDesign.com

Learn more about the Watchon Brand

http://watchon.club

Learn more about Focus Gym ♡ ♡ Be you!

http://focusgymbeyou.com

ONE LAST THING...

If you enjoyed this book or found it entertaining I'd be very grateful if you'd post a short review on Amazon. Your support really does make a difference and I read all the reviews personally so I can get your feedback and make this book even better.

If you'd like to leave a review then all you need to do is review this book on its author's page on Amazon here:

http://amazon.com/author/hunihunfjord

or,

if you have purchased a printed copy of the book, please send your review directly to testimonial@hunihunfjord.com as we would love to include your review on our website.

Thanks again for your support!
Huni Hunfjord